D
Yo

Eve
sp
fav
or
confident by encou
books your child reads with you to the first book
alone, there are I Can Read Books for every stage of r   ding:

SHARED READING
Basic language, word repetition, and whimsical illustrations,
ideal for sharing with your emergent reader

BEGINNING READING
Short sentences, familiar words, and simple concepts
for children eager to read on their own

READING WITH HELP
Engaging stories, longer sentences, and language play
for developing readers

READING ALONE
Complex plots, challenging vocabulary, and high-interest topics
for the independent reader

ADVANCED READING
Short paragraphs, chapters, and exciting themes
for the perfect bridge to chapter books

I Can Read Books have introduced children to the joy of reading
since 1957. Featuring award-winning authors and illustrators and a
fabulous cast of beloved characters, I Can Read Books set the
standard for beginning readers.

A lifetime of discovery begins with the magical words **"I Can Read!"**

V   mation
on   berience.

ISBN-13: 978-0-00-725108-7
ISBN-10: 0-00-725108-4
1 3 5 7 9 10 8 6 4 2

Printed in Italy

I Can Read!

READING
2
WITH HELP

TRANS FORMERS™
MEET THE DECEPTICONS

Adapted by Jennifer Frantz

Illustrations by Guido Guidi

Based on the Screenplay by Roberto Orci & Alex
Kurtzman from a Story by Roberto Orci & Alex Kurtzman
and John Rogers

HarperCollins *Children's Books*

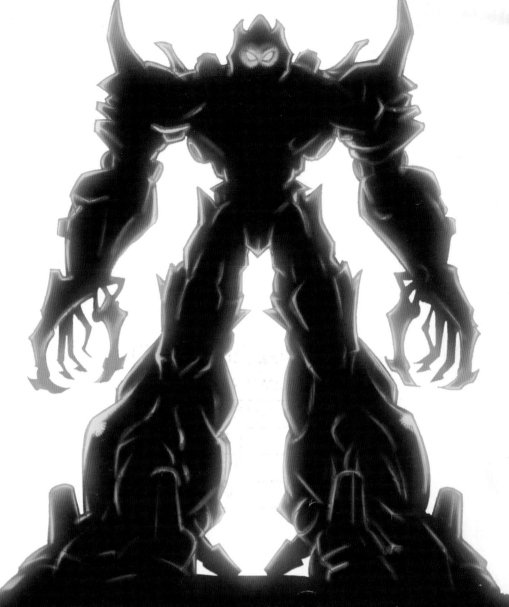

Evil alien robots called Decepticons
have landed on Earth.
They are from the planet Cybertron.

The Decepticons fight

to take over the universe.

They won't stop until they win.

And their next battle

will take place here on Earth.

The Decepticons are Transformers.

They are robots that hide among us.

They pretend to be regular machines.

They are very tricky and very bad.

A friendly chopper comes in for a landing.

But that chopper isn't what it seems.

It turns into a Decepticon named Blackout!

Blackout crushes steel cars.

His blasts wipe out anything in his way.

Blackout is full of nasty surprises.

He carries a robot named Skorponok.

Skorponok digs through the desert sand.

He can sense anything that moves.

He hunts like a scorpion.

He is dangerous.

Frenzy is a Decepticon, too.

He is very tricky.

He can turn into a radio or a boom box.

When he is a robot,

he can shoot metal discs.

Frenzy wants to make big trouble.
He shuts down all the computers
with his terrible scream.

Barricade is another bad guy.

He can transform into a police car.

Frenzy wants to come along.

He turns into the car's CD player.

They drive the streets
looking for trouble.

Megatron is the most powerful

of all Decepticons.

He is a metal giant.

He feeds on energy.

Megatron won't rest

until he finds the Allspark.

It is the Transformers' life force.

Megatron wants it all for himself!

Megatron transforms into

a supersonic jet.

He blasts off on his evil mission.

Megatron finds what he is looking for.

It's the Allspark!

He sends a signal

to the other Decepticons.

Decepticons come

from all over

to help their leader.

The Decepticon named Starscream

jets through the sky.

Bonecrusher and Brawl

rumble over the ground.

The Decepticons unite.

Blackout

Skorponok

Barricade

Frenzy

Together they are a deadly force.

Starscream

Bonecrusher

Who can stop Megatron
and his Decepticon army?
The Autobots!

Autobots are good Transformers.

Their leader is Optimus Prime.

They want to save Earth

from the evil Decepticons.

The battle for the Allspark
and for planet Earth is on.
The metal giants lock in battle.

Megatron takes a hit!

The Decepticons lose this battle!

They flee the planet.

For now the Earth is safc.